D0056110

The Mystery of Too Many Elvises

A Fletcher Mystery

The Mystery of Too Many Elvises

by Elizabeth Levy

Illustrated by Mordicai Gerstein

Aladdin

New York London Toronto Sydney Singapore

To Paula Danziger

First Aladdin Paperbacks edition August 2003
Text copyright © 2003 by Elizabeth Levy
Illustrations copyright © 2003 by Mordicai Gerstein

ALADDIN PAPERBACKS
An imprint of Simon & Schuster Children's Publishing Division
1230 Avenue of the Americas, New York, NY 10020

Also available in an Aladdin paperback edition.
Designed by Lisa Vega
The text of this book was set in ACaslon Regular.

Printed in the United States of America
10 9 8 7 6 5 4 3 2 1

The Library of Congress Control Number for the paperback edition is
2003101089
ISBN 0-689-86157-5 (Aladdin library ed.)

Contents

One

You Ain't Nothing But a Hound Dog

"Sleeping is not a talent," said Jill, looking down at me.

It was a beautiful, warm spring day. I was lying outside under my favorite tree. I opened one eye. I think that knowing oneself is a talent. I am a sleepy basset hound. That's who I am. I don't pretend to be anything else. I don't want to be anything else.

"Fletcher's cute, and he looks like a globe," said Gwen, Jill's best friend.

"It's a pet *talent* show," said Jill. "He's got to have a talent."

"I've got gobs of talent!" Jasper shouted into my ear. Jasper is a flea. He lives on me. When Jill gave me a home, she gave one to Jasper, too.

"Haven't they ever heard of flea circuses?" shouted Jasper. "Watch me fly through the air with the greatest of ease." Jasper swung from the nametag hanging on my collar.

"They can't watch you," I pointed out to him. "They can't even see you."

"Well, at least I'm trying," said Jasper.

Gwen and Jill's school was having a pet talent show. All pets were invited. The problem was that I'm not a show-off. I am a very nice basset hound. I'm smart. But people like "stupid pet tricks," not "smart pet tricks."

And let's face it. I am on the chubby side. Judges don't usually go for my body type.

Finally, I have this stubby tail. It's a perfectly

MY TAIL

fine tail. It's just not the way a basset hound is supposed to look.

Jill threw a Frisbee across the lawn. It sailed against the bright blue sky. "Fetch, Fletcher!" shouted Jill.

REGULAR BASSET TAIL

The Frisbee plopped softly on the grass near me. I sniffed it. It smelled of plastic, not salami. I don't eat plastic. Why should I fetch it? I hated to disappoint Jill, but fetching is just not me.

Jill's mother came out of the back door. "Girls," she said, "do you want lunch? I'm going to have some."

Now *lunch* was a word that I could get behind. I followed Gwen and Jill into the house. Jill's mother had already taken out the peanut butter.

"Anyone for a fried-peanut-butter-and-banana sandwich?" she asked with a grin.

"Mom," said Jill, "that's so disgusting."

"Well, we have some leftover meatloaf if you want that," said Jill's mother.

"Fried peanut butter and banana?" asked Gwen. "I never heard of it."

"It was Elvis Presley's favorite sandwich," said Jill's mother.

Jill rolled her eyes. "Mom loves everything about Elvis. I bet if I had been a boy you would have called me Elvis."

"I did consider Elvisena," teased Jill's mother.

I didn't know anything about Elvis Presley, but peanut butter and banana sounded good to me.

Jill's mother mashed a banana. She mixed it with some peanut butter and then spread it on white bread. Then she melted butter in a frying pan and fried up the sandwich. The smell of slightly crisping peanut butter was tantalizing.

BANANA

BREAD

P-NUT BUTTER + MASHED BANANA

BREAD
BUTTER

P-NUT BUTTER

FRYING PAN

HOW TO MAKE A FRIED P-NUT BUTTER AND MASHED BANANA SANDWICH

I lifted my head and gave a little howl.

Jill's mother smiled down at me. As she hummed a song she cut a piece of her sandwich and gave it to me.

My hips started shaking like a buttercup. I was so happy.

"Look at him," said Jill's mother. "I think Fletcher has a little Elvis in him."

"Mom!" said Jill.

Jill's mother grinned. She took out a CD and put it on. A man with a deep, low voice started singing about a hound dog who never chased a rabbit.

Well, it was true. I have never caught a rabbit. I

think rabbit chasing is as overrated as catching Frisbees. Jill's mom was singing a song about a hound dog just like me! A song for me!

Jill's mother started dancing around the kitchen table. The next song came on. The voice was singing about somebody who was so shook up that he was shaking like a bug.

"This song's about me!" Jasper shrieked so loudly that I jumped up on my hind legs.

"Look at Fletcher!" cried Gwen. "He's shaking just like Elvis. That's his talent. He can be Elvis Presley."

"Oh no," said Jill. "I never wanted a dog that could imitate Elvis."

"But it's so cute," said Gwen. "The judges will love it. Remember when the principal dressed up as Elvis for Fifties Day? We can hook up my little music player to his collar. It'll be Elvis's voice coming out of Fletcher."

I perked up my ears. I did like the boy's singing. Maybe I did have a talent after all.

"I guess I could be Elvis this one time if it'll make Gwen and Jill happy," I whispered to Jasper.

Two

Are You Hungry Tonight?

"I've got just the costume for the talent show," said Jill's mother.

"Oh no, Mom," said Jill. "Not that! It's so embarrassing." Jill's mother left the room.

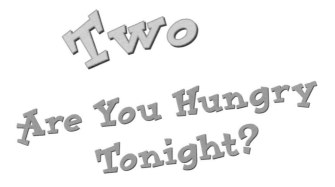

"What is it?" asked Gwen.

Jill's mother came back with a box.

"I kept some of Jill's cute baby clothes," she said. "I just couldn't throw them away. One Halloween when she was a toddler I dressed her up as Elvis Presley."

JILL AS A TODDLER
ELVIS

Jill's mother pulled out a black shiny wig with a pompadour and sideburns. "It's probably got fleas," said Jill.

"Why do humans always say that as if a flea's a bad thing?" complained Jasper.

Gwen put the wig on my head.

It slipped off.

"I can get a little elastic, and I'll make room for his ears," said Jill's mom. "This will work!"

"Mom," protested Jill, "that wig just makes him look silly."

"Wait," said Jill's mother. She looked in the box and came out with a small, shiny jumpsuit with sequins on it and a high collar. Then she took out a big gaudy belt.

"I bet Jill looked adorable in it," said Gwen.

"She was the cutest," said Jill's mother. She held the costume up to me. "I'll have to let it out a little."

She patted me on the belly. "That's okay, Fletcher. Elvis had to have his costumes let out too."

"Mom, you're talking to him as if he understands you."

"He does," said Jill's mother. "Fletcher's sweet, just like Elvis. He loves food. And he's got you two girls loving him. Sounds like Elvis to me."

"Mom, Fletcher is *not* Elvis come back to life."

"You never know," said Jill's mother.

Suddenly there was a song on the CD about somebody in a jailhouse rocking. It reminded me of when I was in the dog pound. My hips started shaking again. I was up on my back feet, shaking my paws.

Jasper was dancing. He remembered what it was like in the pound too. The only way we could cheer ourselves up was to sing. People

JASPER DANCING

thought we were howling, but we were just keeping our spirits up. And this guy, Elvis. I could tell from his singing that he knew. He knew just how we felt.

Jill's mother smiled at me. "Come on, Fletcher," she said. "Let me see if we can get you into this costume." Gwen and Jill held my front paws and got the jumpsuit on me. It was awfully tight.

Jill's mother got out her sewing machine. She kept tapping her feet to the music. She was grinning.

As Jill's mother fixed my costume she talked to Gwen and Jill about Elvis. The more I listened, the more I realized we *did* have a lot in common.

Elvis Aron Presley was born very poor. I was born poor too. I grew up a stray, living on the streets. There's nothing poorer in the dog world than a stray.

Elvis made a promise to his mother that when he grew up they would never be poor or hungry again.

I, too, vowed that if I ever got out of the pound, I would never be hungry again.

Elvis became famous and rich, but he still loved his simple foods! Bacon! Pork rinds! Peanut butter! All delicious! I'm sure he loved salami, too. . . . They just don't write about it as much.

I like simple foods too.

Elvis loved his mommy.

I think of Gwen and Jill as my mommies, and I love them. They feed me salami. I bet Elvis would have loved a salami mommy to pat him on the tummy.

Just thinking about a salami mommy made me smile.

SALAMI MOMMY PATTING ME ON MY TUMMY

"Look at Fletcher," said Gwen. "He looks so happy."

"Maybe he really is Elvis," teased Jill's mother.

From that day on, whenever I heard the opening chords of an Elvis song, I was on my feet, shaking like a bug.

The day before the talent show, Jill's mother came in to watch. "Fletcher has gotten very good," she said.

Jill sighed. "He's not the Beatles, Mom. He's just a hound dog."

"Did you know?" said Jill's mother. "Elvis met the Beatles. He fed them all the southern dishes he had grown up with. Broiled chicken livers, deviled eggs, and sweet-and-sour meatballs. The Beatles said that being with Elvis was the high point of their U.S. tour!"

"Beetles!" exclaimed Jasper. "You mean humans like beetles?"

"It's a rock group," I said. "John, Paul, Ringo, and George."

THE BEETLES

"No Jasper?" asked Jasper. He sounded a little sad.

"Well, maybe they had a pet flea that we don't know about," I told him.

"Beatles, food, songs about a hound dog . . . I think rock and roll is here to stay," said Jasper.

Three

All Shook Up

When Gwen and Jill took me to school for the talent show, I was feeling good. Jill's mother had said that Elvis got his start in a school talent contest when he sang a song about a dog, Old Shep. If Elvis could win by singing about a dog, then maybe a dog could win by singing like Elvis. I wanted to win for Gwen and Jill.

We walked to school. Jill's mother had packed my costume in a bag. We ran into Noah with his cat, Boots, in a carrying case. Boots hissed at me.

"What's your problem?" I asked.

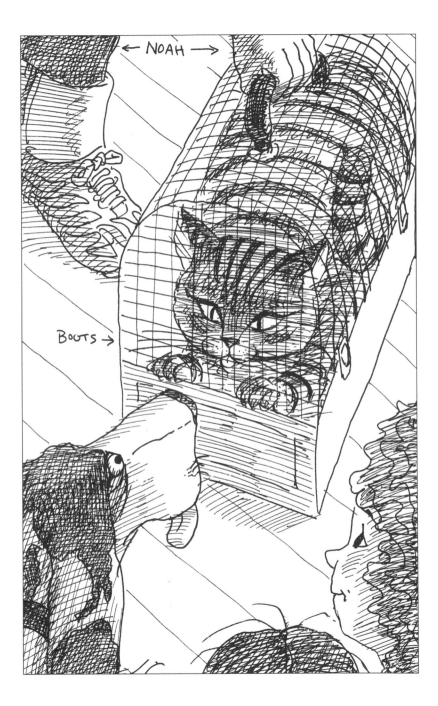

"Nothing personal," said Boots. "I just hate leaving the house. I think I'm going to the vet."

"You're going to a talent show," said Jasper. "Don't you listen to your human?"

"We cats listen to humans as little as possible," said Boots. "I listen to the sound of the can opener. Now *that's* a great sound."

"What's your talent?" I asked.

"I sleep very well in a sunny spot," said Boots.

"Fletcher excels at that," said Jasper.

"You must have something your human finds funny," I said. "Why else would Noah be taking you to the talent show?"

"Oh," said Boots, sounding bored. "I bet you mean that thing where I blow bubbles."

"Blow bubbles!" Jasper shrieked.

"Yeah. Noah holds this round stick in front of me. It looks like a lollipop, but if you blow into it, a shiny bubble floats out. Then I bat it with my paw. I like getting my human to hold the stick for me."

"A stupid human trick," muttered Jasper.

"It sounds cool," I said. I was losing confidence. A fat hound dog pretending to be Elvis wasn't the same as a cat that could blow bubbles.

When we got to the school auditorium I could hardly hear myself think. There were so many kids and animals—parrots, gerbils, rabbits, and even a tarantula.

"He dances on eight legs," said the spider's proud owner, Sam. "He's had the poison taken out of him."

Gwen and Jill left me to go fill out a card which would tell the judges my name and my talent.

"I recite the Gettysburg Address," said a parrot in a loud, clear human voice. "They put me in a tall hat, so I look like Abe Lincoln. I'm just glad it's a short speech. Two hundred and seventy two words.

'Four score and seven years ago our fathers brought forth on this continent, a new nation, conceived in Liberty and dedicated to the proposition that all men are created equal.'"

"That's beautiful," I said.

"Thanks. My name is Quixote."

"You're amazing!" I said. "You can use human speech."

"It's a bit of a burden," said Quixote. "I usually only give them a few words at a time. Otherwise humans would want me to talk to them all the time. There's nothing humans like to do more than talk."

"They like to eat," I pointed out.

"Yes," said Quixote, "but most animals eat without chatting. Humans can't chew without a chat."

"You know, I never realized that," I admitted.

"Well, I've lived a long time," said Quixote. "I've

been watching humans longer than any of you. Look how excited they get when I say, 'Quixote wants a cracker.'"

Natan, Quixote's owner, grinned. He reached into a plastic bag and pulled out a cracker.

"That's it?" I said. "No begging? You just say the words and you get a cracker! Now that's a talent."

Quixote nodded his noble parrot head at me. "Parrots have lived with humans for thousands of years. Did you know that the kings in the Caribbean gave Columbus gifts of parrots?"

"You sure know a lot," I said.

"Well, we parrots live a very long time. I'm already fifty years old."

"Fifty years old!" I exclaimed. "You were alive when Elvis was alive!"

"Ah, yes, indeed," said Quixote. He began to squawk out, "Love Me Tender."

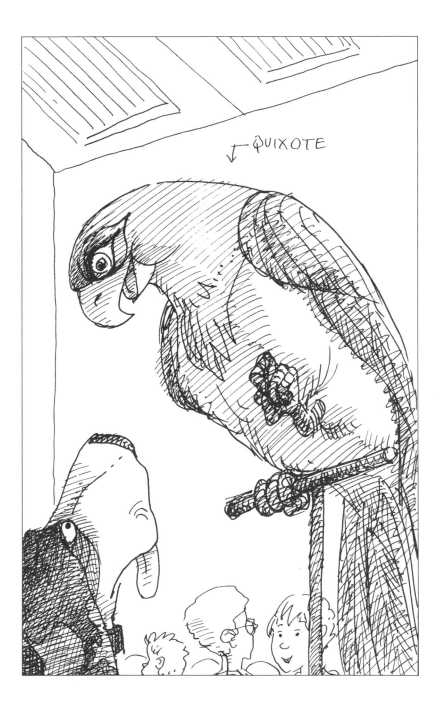

"Uh-oh," whispered Jasper. "Another Elvis. . . ."

"*Moi?* An Elvis impersonator?" said Quixote. "Don't be silly. It would be beneath my dignity."

"Fletcher doesn't worry about dignity," said Jasper as if it were something to be proud of.

Suddenly something stung me on the rear end. "Jasper!" I yelled. "Did you bite me?"

"Me? Never!" said Jasper.

"Well, one of your relatives just landed," I said. I was mad. Jasper and I had a deal: He lived on me and he kept other fleas off.

"Ouch!" I yelled. Another flea bit me on the butt.

"Whoops! Sorry!" I heard a squeaky voice say. It didn't sound like a flea.

I looked around. A gerbil was holding a rubber band in its paws, ready to let it fly. "I wasn't aiming at you, but you *do* have a big target there."

"What are you doing?" I demanded.

"Practicing my act," said the gerbil. "Is that Australia on your hip?"

"It is," I said.

"It makes a great target," said the gerbil.

"It's not a target. It's my rear end."

"Sorry. It's my act. I fling rubber bands," said the gerbil. "Hi, my name's Otis."

"You can fling rubber bands?" I was shocked. "I never heard of an animal doing that."

"I've got the little paws to do it," said Otis. "Put one on my claws, and I can make it fly. So what's your talent?"

"Yes," said Quixote, in a very cultured voice. "What is your talent, my finely furred hound dog?"

All the animals were looking at me.

"Tell them," squeaked Jasper. "Don't be shy!"

I felt my confidence oozing out of me, like a used-up jar of peanut butter.

"Uh . . . I can eat and dance like Elvis Presley," I said.

"What did Elvis eat?" asked Quixote.

"Bananas and peanut butter, meatloaf . . . just about anything that wasn't nailed down," I said. "Elvis liked meatloaf because he could swallow it faster than steak."

"That's not a talent," said a big bulldog. "That's gluttony."

"Fletcher can shake and dance like Elvis," said Jasper, trying to stand up for me. "It's a lot harder than it looks. So what's your talent?"

"I'd rather not say," said the bulldog. "You never know who will steal your act."

"This talent show is just for fun," I said.

"Show business is not for scaredy cats," said the

bulldog. "It's a tough business. My name is Parker, by the way. Colonel Parker."

"It's just a grade school talent show," I said.

"A grade school talent show is only the beginning," said Parker. "Pets are big right now. Haven't you heard of *Animal Planet*? The human world is always looking for a good animal act."

"Like a gerbil flinging rubber bands," said Otis excitedly.

Just then Gwen came up with her music player. "Hi, Fletcher," she said. "I just want to make sure that I get the sound level right."

When she put the music on, I couldn't help myself. I just had to shake. Over in the bleachers some kids started to clap. "Look at that Elvis!" cried one.

"He's so cute," cried another kid.

"And look, he's got that big dog dancing too! He's just too cute. I love him."

I wondered what big dog they were talking about. Then I turned around to see one of the largest greyhounds I had ever seen. He was up on his hind legs, and he was dancing too.

The kids started clapping for us both. I heard one boy say, "Those two dogs are rockin'."

Gwen was grinning. "It works fine," she said. "Stay here, Fletcher. Jill and I will be right back." She took off the music player and put it on a bench.

"I like that music," said the big greyhound.

I looked up at him. He was the kind of dog that could have me for breakfast.

"What's your name?" he asked.

"Fletcher!" I barked. "What's yours?" I didn't want him to know that I was afraid of him. Big dogs scare me, but you can't let them know you're afraid.

"I'm Ringo!" he said in a voice so low it sounded like a growl.

"Ringo! Like the Beatles?" asked Jasper.

"Is that a flea on your rear?" asked Ringo. "And does he dare to talk to you?"

"That flea is my buddy," I said, sticking up for Jasper the way he had stuck up for me.

"Keep him away from me!" warned Ringo. "Or I'll take a bite out of him."

"I'm all shook up," taunted Jasper, doing a triple flip.

"Stop your flips, you little flea," demanded Ringo.

"I'm not a little flea—I flip for Elvis. Do you know the songs of Elvis Presley?" Jasper asked.

"I'm Ringo! Named for Ringo Starr of the Beatles. My owner doesn't listen to Elvis much."

"What's your talent?" asked Jasper.

"I can play the drums," said Ringo. "My owner

flips a drumstick into the air. I catch it and beat the drum."

"Drumstick!" I said excitedly. "You mean like a turkey drumstick?"

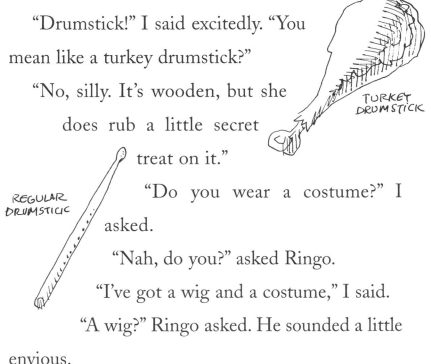

TURKEY DRUMSTICK

REGULAR DRUMSTICK

"No, silly. It's wooden, but she does rub a little secret treat on it."

"Do you wear a costume?" I asked.

"Nah, do you?" asked Ringo.

"I've got a wig and a costume," I said.

"A wig?" Ringo asked. He sounded a little envious.

"Well, Elvis had a real distinctive hairdo," I said. "Lots of people copied it."

"Ringo Starr had the best mop-top of all the Beatles," said Ringo thoughtfully. "Maybe my owner should have made me a wig."

My leg started twitching. "What's wrong with you?" whispered Jasper.

"'All Shook Up' isn't just a song," I told him. "I'm nervous. I never realized there would be so many talented pets."

"That's because you haven't got on your wig and your costume," said Jasper. "Once you have them on, you'll be great!"

But I didn't feel great. I was so nervous my stomach was all shook up!

Four

Heartbreak Hotel

Mr. Philips, the music teacher, hit a big gong. "Children, get your acts ready. We're going to start soon. I'm glad so many of you have come. This is a very exciting event. Our first pet talent show!"

"Fletcher, you've got to win," said Jill.

I rolled my eyes. As if I wasn't feeling enough pressure already. I wondered if the real Elvis was ever as nervous as I was. Maybe that's why he shook so much when he was on stage.

I sighed. I could have used a little nap. Maybe Elvis took naps too.

Gwen and Jill took me into a corner and started to put on my costume. Noah was there with Boots. They were practicing blowing bubbles.

"Way cool!" said Gwen admiringly.

"What does Fletcher do?" Noah asked. "So far all I've seen him do is sleep."

"He imitates Elvis," said Jill.

"It's not just what he does," explained Gwen. "When he's got his costume on it's as if he *is* Elvis."

"This I got to see," said Noah.

Jill reached into the bag. She pulled out the jumpsuit. As Gwen and Jill put the jumpsuit on me, I could feel my confidence returning. I flexed my muscles in my Elvis suit. The sequins glimmered. Normally, I'm kind of shy and quiet. But in this suit, well, I felt like a king. Now I just needed the hair, and I'd be stylin'.

Then Gwen looked in the bag. "You forgot it!" she shouted at Jill.

"Forgot what?" asked Jill, straightening my big beaded belt.

"His wig," said Gwen. "It's not here."

"Oh no!" screeched Jasper. "You need the wig!"

"It's got to be there," said Jill. "Mom put it in first. I saw her put it in the bottom of the bag."

"Well, it's not here now," muttered Gwen. She began to tap her braces. "I think somebody took our wig to ruin Fletcher's act."

Gwen tapped her braces again. She looked around the gymnasium. "See that parrot dressed up as Abe Lincoln? Maybe Natan stole our wig to make a beard for him."

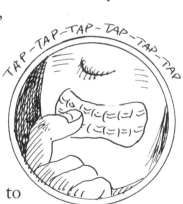

GWEN TAPPING HER BRACES

"As Elvis you outshine any parrot," whispered

Jasper. "But you really need your wig. Without it you just look like a chubby basset hound in a silly jumpsuit."

I knew Jasper didn't realize how much his words hurt me.

Gwen and Jill dragged me by my leash over to Quixote and Natan.

Quixote looked down at me with a world-weary gaze.

Gwen tapped her braces.

She studied Quixote's beard. Quixote looked bored.

"What are you looking at?" asked Natan.

"Why is your parrot wearing a beard?" she asked.

"Because Abe Lincoln had a beard," said Natan. "It's part of Quixote's act. My mom made it for me."

"Did she?" asked Gwen. "Or did you steal our Elvis wig to make a beard?"

I studied the wig on Quixote's beard. It had strands of gray in it, sticking out from his bright orange beak. My Elvis wig had no gray in it. My Elvis wig was as jet-black as the shoe polish that Elvis used to put on his hair.

I tugged on Jill's hand.

"Fletcher is trying to tell us something," said Jill.

Sometimes I wish I was a parrot and could just speak to humans in words they could understand.

"What is it, boy?" Gwen asked me.

I didn't want her to blame Quixote and Natan. I tried to bark out to her that she should look closer at the wig.

"He just wants his wig back," said Gwen. She pulled at Quixote's beard.

"Hands off!" shouted Quixote in a loud voice. But he was careful not to bite her. I had to respect that elderly parrot.

"That's not my wig," I whispered to Jasper. "Gwen is trying to beard the wrong bird. Natan and Quixote didn't take my wig."

Gwen was arguing with Natan. When she argues, she has to tap her braces. Jill was arguing too. When Jill argues she likes to talk with her hands. Even monkeys don't talk with their hands as much as humans. Jill dropped the leash to poke her finger at Natan.

"Come on," I whispered to Jasper. "Let's make tracks. We'll have to find the wig ourselves. Gwen and Jill will never leave Quixote alone."

"Maybe that dog Ringo took it," said Jasper. "He said that the real Ringo had famous hair, and he seemed to be a little jealous of you."

I scratched behind my ear. "That's not a bad idea."

"Careful," said Jasper. "That's where I'm sitting." He jumped to my other side.

I wiggled.

There were a bunch of second graders in the corner. They began to giggle. "That Elvis hound dog is just *soooo* cute," they said. "I love Elvis."

I heard a low growl. Colonel Parker, the bulldog, was behind the bleachers practicing his secret act.

"Don't growl at little kids," I said to him. "It scares them."

"Those kids seemed to like you," Parker said. "You and I should talk. Put together a little act. With my brains . . . and your cute pudginess . . . I could manage things for you."

I wasn't sure that I liked that crack about my cute pudginess.

"Who do you think you are, talking to Fletcher like that?" demanded Jasper.

"Well, he is a colonel," I said.

"Of what?" Jasper asked.

"It's a name of respect, little flea," said the colonel. "Something that you could use a little more of. Now, what do you say, Fletcher? Do you want me to be your manager?"

"Fletcher's already got me," said Jasper. "I manage his talent just fine."

"Yeah, with you," sneered the colonel, "that dog will end up in a fleabag hotel. Heartbroken and poor."

"First of all," said Jasper, "some of my relatives live in fleabag hotels. And Fletcher is never

FLEABAG HOTEL

HEARTBREAK HOTEL

going to end up in the Heartbreak Hotel. Don't worry about it."

"Thanks for the offer, colonel, sir," I said. "But I'm not much for marching and taking orders.

Even from Jill and her best friend, Gwen, and I love them."

"You could learn a lot from a dog like me," said the colonel.

Just then Colonel Parker's owner, Tom, came over with Gwen and Jill. "There you are, Parker," he said.

"Fletcher!" said Gwen. "We looked closer at Quixote's wig. It wasn't yours."

Suddenly a little girl named Ella came up. "Have you seen Ringo?" she cried to Gwen and Jill. "I can't find him anywhere. I've got his drumstick ready."

"What did Ringo look like again?" Jill asked. "There are so many pets."

"He's a big greyhound," said Ella.

"Oh, I think I just saw him," said Tom.

"Where?" asked Ella.

"He was backstage," said Tom. "He had something in his mouth."

Just then there was an announcement from the stage. "Girls and boys. Please come forward when your name is called, and get your number for when you and your pet will appear."

The owners all ran to the center of the stage.

"Come on," I said to Jasper. "I have a feeling that when we find that oversized greyhound we'll find my wig, too!"

Five

Don't Be Cruel

We ran backstage. The tarantula was practicing its tarantella. Otis was flinging rubber bands. "Have you seen Ringo?" we asked every pet we saw. No one knew where Ringo was.

I sniffed the air. Very faintly, I smelled salami.

"Salami," I said to Jasper.

"Forget salami," said Jasper.

"Who could ever forget salami?" I asked. "If only people thought smelling salami was a good trick, I would ace this talent show."

I kept sniffing. Over by the edge of the stage

was a little building that looked like a gingerbread house. It must have been used in a play about fairy tales. But it didn't smell like gingerbread. It smelled like salami.

The little house had a window made of cellophane. The door had an old fashioned lock to it—just an old board between two metal brackets—but the board was higher than my head.

I tried to gaze through the window. It was wrinkled and cloudy. I thought I saw something that looked like a bat flying inside.

"Bats," whispered Jasper. "Bat fleas are not any-

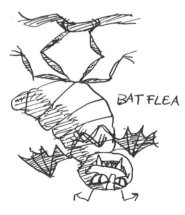

BAT FLEA

thing you want to meet up with. They're our nastiest relatives."

"Have you ever met a bat that smelled like salami?" I asked him.

"No," said Jasper. "Stop talking about salami! We're supposed to be finding your wig. You're going to have to go on stage any minute now."

"I definitely smell salami in that little house," I said. "I can't help myself. Where salami goes I must follow."

We heard a faint howl coming from the little house.

"What's in that thing?" asked Jasper. "Was it a prop for *Little Shop of Horrors*?"

I heard a pounding.

"Get me out of here." I heard a low growl. It sounded like a greyhound.

"Ringo?" I asked.

"Who's there?"

"Me, Fletcher," I said. "What are you doing in there? Ella is looking for you!"

"I found something that smelled like salami. I

thought it was a mouse made out of salami. Salami is what Ella rubs on my drumstick. I love salami."

"Mice aren't made out of a salami," I said.

MOUSE MADE OF SALAMI

"You never know what humans will make food look like," said Ringo. "Haven't you seen those animal crackers they eat?"

He had a point.

"But this house is too small for me. I got in, but I can't seem to get out," said Ringo. "Help me."

I pushed against the door. It wouldn't budge.

"You're locked in," I said.

"It's just a storybook house," said Jasper. "You can blow it down."

"Stand back!" I warned.

I took a running start. I don't run often, but when I do, I can put on quite a surprising burst of speed.

I pushed at the door with my shoulder. It barely budged.

I jumped. The piece of wood in the metal brackets holding the door shut was too high up.

"Hey," said Jasper. "I've got an idea. There's a hockey stick in the corner. What if you took it and put it under that piece of wood. Then if we pushed up on it, it might move the board."

"What's that flea going on about?" asked Ringo. "A flea never had a good idea in his life."

"Don't underestimate the mind of a flea," I said. "That's one smart flea who lives with me. He's got a great idea."

I went and got the hockey stick and I did what Jasper suggested. I put it under the board blocking the door.

"Okay, now jump on it!" shouted Jasper.

"Are you actually doing what a flea says?"

growled Ringo from inside the house.

"Hush up!" I said. "We're doing this for you. Don't be cruel to a flea that's trying to help you!"

I jumped. The wooden board budged. But it didn't move.

"Do it again!" said Jasper. "This time I'll jump too."

"Fleas don't weigh anything," I reminded Jasper.

"Let's just try it," said Jasper. "On the count of three, jump!"

Jasper shouted, "One, two, three." I jumped with all my might and so did Jasper. I couldn't believe it. The hockey stick flipped the board holding the door.

"We did it!" I shouted.

I went flying inside. I landed right at Ringo's feet. My wig was in his mouth.

"That's mine!" I shouted. "You took it because you wanted a wig just like mine."

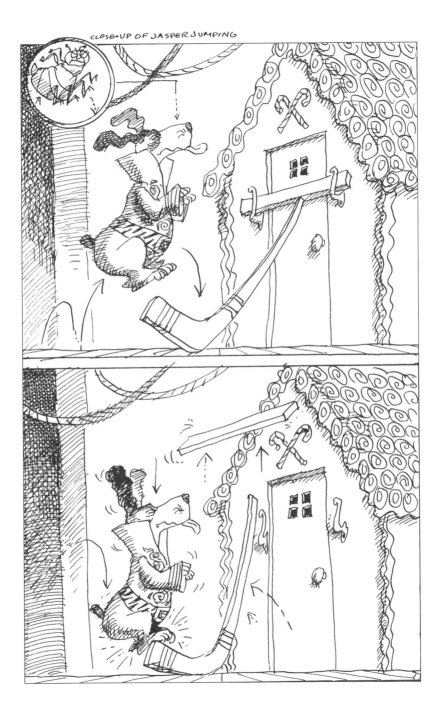

"It smelled of salami," said Ringo. "Someone said there was salami in a sack. I'm a sucker for salami."

"Who told you there was salami in a sack?" I asked.

"I can't remember. It wasn't a human. But I met so many new pets here today. I can't keep them straight."

"Give me back the wig!" I said.

Ringo dropped it. "It didn't taste good," he said. "It's hairy."

"It probably smelled of salami because that's my favorite food," I said.

"It's mine too!" he said. "At least we have that in common."

Gwen and Jill came running backstage with Ella. "There's Ringo!" said Ella.

"And there's Fletcher's Elvis wig," cried Jill.

"The mystery is solved," said Gwen. "Ringo took our Elvis's wig. And Fletcher followed him out here and got it back. Good dog, Fletcher!"

"Well, that turned out to be a tempest in a teapot," said Jasper. "All's well that ends well."

"Thank you for rescuing me," whispered Ringo. "You're not such a bad flea. And Fletcher, if you ever want to flip the drumsticks with me, you're my man."

TEMPEST IN A TEAPOT

Ringo trotted off behind Ella. He glanced back at me and wagged his tail.

"Well, I have to say, he was quite polite at the end," said Jasper.

"Yes, I believe the real Ringo is very polite too, but we still have a mystery to solve," I said.

"What mystery?" asked Jasper. "Ringo took your

wig. He didn't want it for himself. You must have gotten salami on it, and he smelled it. Mystery solved."

"No, it's not solved," I said. "Somebody tried to keep Ringo from the contest by locking him inside that little house backstage. And somebody told him to take my wig."

I knew the mystery wasn't solved. But just then there was a gong from inside the assembly room. The talent show was going to start. All I had to do was hope that nothing more would go wrong.

Six

Love Me Tender

The first act in the talent show was Sam's tarantula. Sam put his spider on an overhead projector so that every move it made showed up on the screen. That tarantula was quite amazing. The tarantula did a tarantella on the overhead projector. Everybody could see his eight hairy legs moving on the screen to the sounds of the Italian music.

The whole audience gasped when the spider slipped off the screen. It looked like he was escaping. Sam had to grab him and put him in back in the box.

I didn't think he was going to win the talent contest.

Next up was Boots. Her owner held up the stick, and Boots actually blew the bubbles through. Then she batted them with her paw. The crowd went wild. I knew she was going to be tough competition.

Jill's mother came over to Gwen and Jill. "I cleaned Fletcher's wig and dried it with the hand dryers in the teachers' bathroom," she said.

"Thanks, Mom," said Jill.

Jill's mother put the wig on me. She adjusted it so a curl hung low over my eyes. "There," she whispered into my ear. "You look perfect."

I didn't feel perfect. I wished that my stomach wasn't quite so all shook up. I knew that there was some creature out there who had it in for me, especially when I was Elvis. But I didn't know what to do.

On stage, Otis flung his rubber bands, but they were a little hard to see. I waited nervously, panting.

"You'll be on soon," Jill whispered to me.

Otis finished his rubber bands to polite applause.

Mr. Philips came out on stage. "Well, that was very unusual," he said. Otis let go of another rubber band and it hit Mr. Philip's bald head.

Mr. Philips laughed, but not very heartily.

"Okay, folks, for our next treat," he looked at his card, "we have Ringo on the drums!"

Ringo bounded onstage to the tune of "A Hard Day's Night." Ella threw a drumstick, and he caught it with all four feet off the ground.

The crowed cheered. Ringo was a treat. He was going to be hard to beat.

Mr. Philips came back on stage. He looked at his next card. "Well, I guess you can't have too much rock and roll. Our next act is Fletcher singing "You

Ain't Nothing But a Hound Dog," as Elvis!"

Jill pushed me on stage. Gwen turned on the music player. But it wasn't Elvis. Instead, a sweet girlish voice began singing, "How much is that doggy in the window?" It had no beat. You couldn't dance to it.

I just stood there. My hips couldn't swivel. I didn't know what to do. I'm not a doggy-in-the-window type. I'm Elvis.

I lay down and put my feet in the air. The crowd politely applauded, but they didn't get it, and neither did I. This wasn't my act. My act had been sabotaged.

Gwen and Jill came running onstage. They explained to Mr. Philips that somehow the wrong music had come on. Mr. Philips agreed to give them another chance.

Gwen was tapping her braces. "This isn't my music player. Somebody switched it," she whispered to Jill. We had to get off the stage.

Mr. Philips announced the next act. "Tom's bull-dog, Colonel Parker, has a musical number he's going to do for you."

Suddenly we could all hear the strains of "You Ain't Nothing But a Hound Dog!" But it was coming out of the wrong dog!

The bulldog Parker was standing on his hind feet, trying to move his hips. But he didn't have any rhythm. He had no soul.

I bounded on stage and knocked him down.

"I know Elvis and you're no Elvis!" I growled at him. "You knew your act wasn't going anywhere, so you tried to steal mine."

Just then a voice shouted from backstage. It was Tom, Parker's owner. "The music players must have gotten mixed up," said Tom. "I'm sorry. It was an accident."

I looked at the bulldog. "It was no accident, was it?" I growled to Parker.

Parker didn't do anything. He lay there like a dog playing possum. I didn't trust him. "First you tried to get rid of my wig by telling Ringo there was salami in the bag. And you locked Ringo in that little house, because you saw the kids liked him. Bulldogs have the strongest necks and teeth in the dog world. You're taller than me, and you were able to get that board in the brackets. When we got Ringo out, next you tried to switch music. But you can't be Elvis. You're not the real thing. I am. There's such a thing as too many Elvises, and you're one Elvis too many."

"Look, Fletcher," whispered Parker. "Forget this grade school talent show. I admit you've got a good act going there. The kids loved just watching you rehearse. It's a waste to use your talent on a grade school. We could go places."

"I don't want to go places," I said to him. "I love Gwen and Jill. I just want to be Elvis for them. And then I'll go back to being me. . . ."

"You idiot!" exploded Parker. "Don't you see where we could go with this! You could be an American idol."

I grinned at him. "I am an American idle," I said. "I like to sleep. And eat. But for today I've got to shake, rattle, and roll."

"Hey," said Jasper. "Maybe we should have listened to him. You've got a talent. It could be bigger than this place."

I went up to Gwen and Jill.

"Fletcher," said Jill, putting her arms around me.

"This is where we belong," I whispered to Jasper.

"Mr. Philips!" Gwen shouted. "Our act is ready!" She hooked the music player to my collar.

I took center stage. Elvis's voice came out. My

hips started shaking. The kids started clapping with me. I could feel the power pulsing through me! My legs were shaking as wild as a bug!

Even Mr. Philips was grinning and dancing!

I won, paws down.

For the finale, Mr. Philips invited all the pets and their owners on stage for a final bowwow. The music came on. The owners sang "Love Me Tender," and we pets all chimed in with our chirps, meows, and howls. Somehow it all harmonized. Even Quixote bobbed his noble parrot head. All except Colonel Parker. He was sulking in a corner. He just would never get the soul of Elvis.